THE SHOELACE SOLUTION

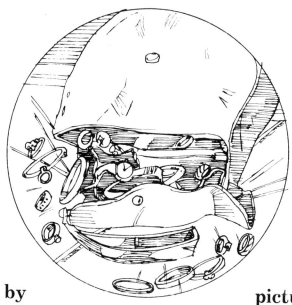

written by
Ray Broekel

pictures by
Dave Brandon

CAROLRHODA BOOKS

MINNEAPOLIS, MINNESOTA U.S.A.

A
CAROLRHODA
MINI-
MYSTERY

International Standard Book Number: 0-87614-115-7
Library of Congress Catalog Card Number: 79-52409

1 2 3 4 5 6 7 8 9 10 85 84 83 82 81 80

"Darn these sneakers," Mark Murphy said to himself. "They just will not stay tied." *Snap.* The shoelace broke off in his hand. "Oh, darn again!"

Mark was standing at the bus stop. He was waiting for Liz Harris. They were going to the museum. There was an American Indian show there. They both wanted to see it.

Liz came running up the street. "Hi, Mark," she said. "Sorry I'm late."

"That's O.K.," said Mark. "You don't have a shoelace on you, do you?" He pointed to his sneaker.

"No," said Liz. "But there's a shoe store just up the street."

The shoe store was just a block away. "That's funny," said Liz when they got there. "What's a shoe store doing with jewelry in the window?"

They went inside. Mark asked the saleswoman for one new shoelace.

"New shoelaces are sold in pairs," she said.

"But I only need one," said Mark.

The woman smiled. "I have a box of old laces in the back. Maybe I can find one for you."

"Thank you," said Mark. He turned to Liz.

"Look at that man over there," she said. "He must be trying on every shoe in the store. See all those boxes beside him?"

The saleswoman came back with a shoe-lace. "Try this one," she said.

Mark sat down across from a woman holding a very large pocketbook. She had on bright red shoes. She was about to try on some bright green shoes. Mark smiled.

"I said brown, not black." An old woman next to Mark was yelling at a salesman.

What a funny place, Mark thought. He leaned over to lace his shoe. "Just right," he said to the saleswoman. "How much does it cost?"

"No charge." The saleswoman smiled. "Just remember us when you need a new pair."

"I will," said Mark.

As he and Liz left, Liz looked again at the man trying on all the shoes. She shook her head. "The salesman just brought him three more boxes."

"I'll race you to the bus stop," said Mark. The two of them took off. Liz won. Mark wasn't even close. He was half a block behind. Liz walked back to him. "You sure are easy to beat," she said. "What happened?"

"My other shoelace broke," Mark answered. "It's back to the shoe store for me."

"Maybe you should buy a pair of loafers," said Liz.

"Very funny," said Mark. "Are you coming?"

"No," said Liz. "I'll wait here."

THE SHOELACE
SOLUTION

Mark started back. He was almost there when a man nearly ran into him. It was the man who had been trying on all the shoes. He wasn't carrying any boxes. After all that he didn't even buy anything, Mark thought. But he sure is in a hurry.

Mark went into the store. The woman who had given him the shoelace laughed. "Don't tell me," she said. "Let me guess. The other lace broke. Right?"

Mark got out some change. "This time I'll buy a new pair," he said.

The woman handed him some new shoe-laces. "Do you remember any of the people who were in here before?" she asked.

"Sure," Mark answered. "I just ran into one of them. Why?"

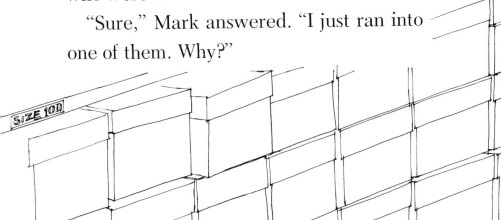

"We're having a special jewelry sale," she said. She pointed to a tray of jewelry on the counter. It was half empty. "We think one of those people stole some jewelry."

Mark described the people he remembered. Then he left to meet Liz. "Guess what?" he said to her. He told her about the robbery.

"I bet it was that man," she said.

"Maybe," said Mark. "He sure was in a hurry. I ran into him on my way back."

"Or it could have been that lady sitting next to you," said Liz. "She sure was mean."

"You can say that again," said Mark.
"Hey! There's our bus!"

The two of them ran to the bus stop. They got there just in time. An old woman was getting on. She was holding two shopping bags.

Liz poked Mark. The lady was the one who had been in the shoe store.

Mark and Liz got on the bus. They paid their fares and walked to the back. The woman with the shopping bags had found a seat.

"Should we follow her?" Liz asked.

"I don't know," said Mark. "She looks suspicious all right. But so did that man who was in such a hurry."

"Well, she's on the bus. The man isn't," Liz said.

Four stops later the woman got up. She went to the door.

"That solves one problem," said Liz. "This is our stop. Come on."

"What do we do now?" Mark asked.

"Follow her, I guess," said Liz. "She's going our way anyway. Maybe we'll think of something."

The woman hurried away. At the end of two long blocks she went into an apartment house.

"I guess that's that," Mark said. "I'll write the address down. Then we might as well go." Suddenly Mark stopped short. "Liz, I don't believe this. Look up ahead."

Liz saw a woman half a block in front of them. She was wearing bright red shoes.

"I think that woman was in the shoe store too," Mark said. "She was sitting across from me. I noticed her shoes and her pocketbook."

"It sure is a big one," Liz said. "And it really looks full. Maybe we were wrong about the other two. What do you think?"

"I think we should get closer," Mark said. "I'm not positive it's the same woman. I need to see her face."

"There's a policeman on the next corner," Liz said. "Wait until we're almost there. Then get ahead of her."

Mark laughed. "Even if she is the same woman, we don't know that she stole the jewelry."

"Well, just in case," said Liz.

They followed the woman almost to the corner. Then Mark ran ahead. He was just about to pass her when he tripped. He bumped into her. Her pocketbook flew out of her hand. It hit the ground and came open. Jewelry fell out all over the place.

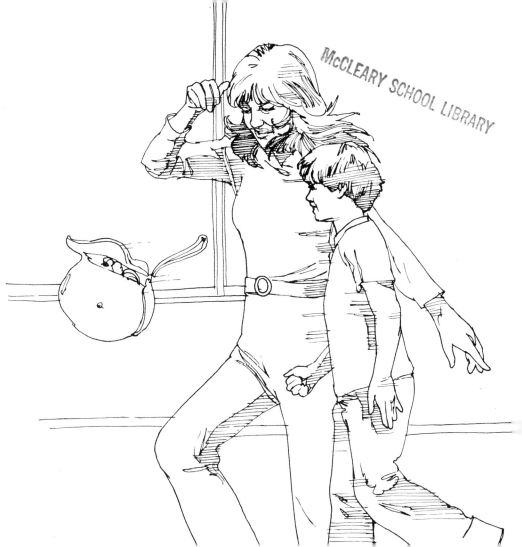

The policeman came running over. "Can I help you?" he asked. The woman had picked up her pocketbook. She was putting the jewelry back into it. The policeman looked suspicious. "That's a lot of jewelry you have there," he said. "Can I ask why you are carrying it around with you?"

"It's my sister's," the woman said. "I borrowed it from her for a trip I was taking. Now I'm returning it to her."

"That's not true!" Mark burst out. "She stole it!" He told the policeman about the robbery. The policeman took Mark's name and address and the name and address of the store. Then he turned to the woman.

"I think you had better come along with me," he said.

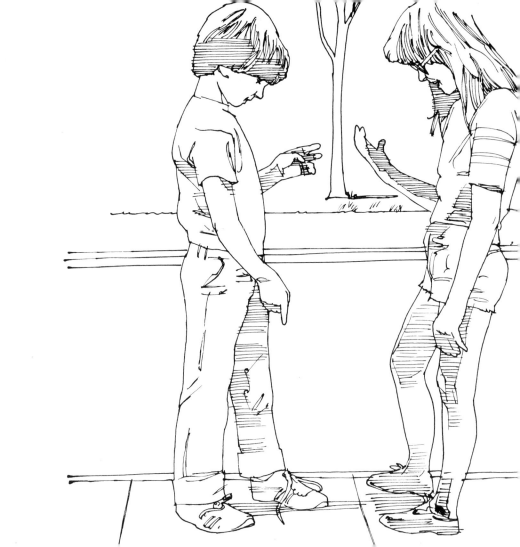

Liz looked at Mark after it was all over. "Did you bump into her on purpose?" she asked.

Mark laughed. "No," he said. "Remember those new shoelaces I bought?"

"Sure."

"Well, one of them came untied. I tripped over it. That's when I bumped into the woman."

Liz pushed her sunglasses back up on her nose. "Ever heard of Sherlock Holmes?" she asked.

"He was a great detective," Mark answered.

Liz began to laugh. "Well, from now on you have a new name," she said. "I'm going to call you *Shoelace* Holmes!"